This

MoshiMoshiKawaii ®

book belongs to

....

....

Meet the Moshi
and all their friends!

Cherry Blossom Moshi   **Cherry Blossom Moshi's** Friends

Green Moshi   **Green Moshi's** Friends

Bee Moshi   **Bee Moshi's** Friends

Speckled Moshi   **Speckled Moshi's** Friends

Aloha Moshi   **Aloha Moshi's** Friends

Mermaid Moshi   **Mermaid Moshi's** Friends

Submarine Moshi   **Submarine Moshi's** Friends

Baby Moshi   **Baby Moshi's** Friends

Pineapple Moshi   **Pineapple Moshi's** Friends

Rainbow Moshi   **Rainbow Moshi's** Friends

Star Moshi   **Star Moshi's** Friends

Angel Moshi   **Angel Moshi's** Friends

Strawberry Moshi   **Strawberry Moshi's** Friends

Super Moshi   **Super Moshi's** Friends

Polka Dot Moshi   **Polka Dot Moshi's** Friends

Lovely Moshi   **Lovely Moshi's** Friends

Chef Moshi   **Chef Moshi's** Friends

Princess Moshi   **Princess Moshi's** Friends

Clover Moshi   **Clover Moshi's** Friends

Sari Moshi   **Sari Moshi's** Friends

Baby Prince Moshi   **Baby Prince Moshi's** Friends

Waitress Moshi   **Waitress Moshi's** Friends

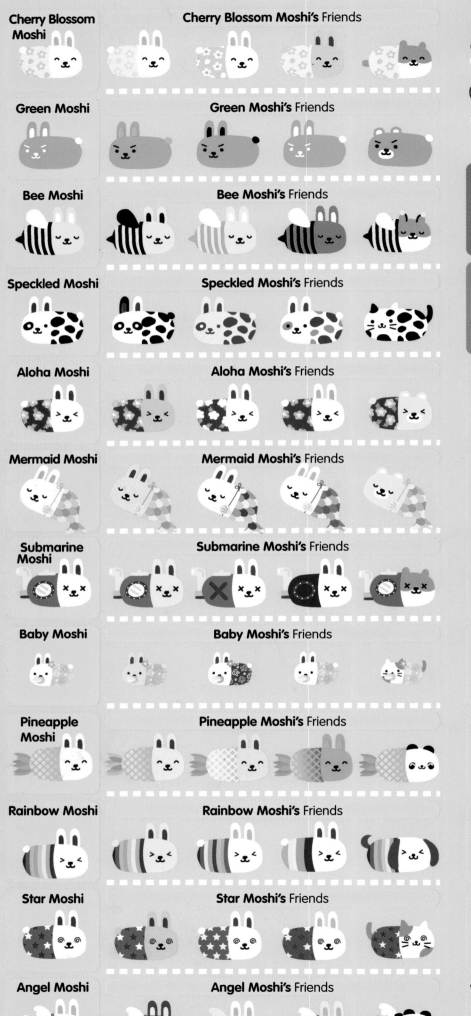

At first glance, all the Moshi look the same. Look again and you'll see they are all different! Find each type in the book.

Cherry Moshi

Plaid Moshi

Fluffy Moshi

Silk Moshi

Racing Moshi

Robot Moshi

Airplane Moshi

Rocket Moshi

Bus Moshi
Bus Moshi's Friends

Ambulance Moshi
Ambulance Moshi's Friends

Injury Moshi
Injury Moshi's Friends

Flower Moshi
Flower Moshi's Friends

Kindergarten Moshi
Kindergarten Moshi's Friends

High School Moshi
High School Moshi's Friends

Arabesque Moshi
Arabesque Moshi's Friends

Giraffe Moshi
Giraffe Moshi's Friends

Hedgehog Moshi
Hedgehog Moshi's Friends

Fish Moshi
Fish Moshi's Friends

Panda Moshi
Panda Moshi's Friends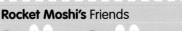

Firefly Moshi
Firefly Moshi's Friends

Moshi Town is a wonderland teeming with all sorts of cute Moshi dressed up in colorful outfits.

Strawberry Moshi is looking for her sweetheart, **Super Moshi**, but Moshi Town is so busy that she will need your help to find him.

Strawberry Moshi   **Super Moshi**

Strawberry Moshi and **Super Moshi** are in every scene. Find them in busy Moshi Town. Look carefully, because there are Moshi who look almost the same as **Strawberry Moshi** and **Super Moshi**.

See what other funny Moshi you can find in each picture. Take a close look at their faces and the clothes they are wearing. Look out for the giant Maze Moshi in the middle of the story!

At the end of the book, there are more Moshi for you to go back and look for. Find out what adventures they have been on.

There are even different Moshi on the front and back covers. Can you find them in the pictures too?

MoshiMoshiKawaii ® is a registered trademark.
Original Japanese edition published by GAKKEN Co. Ltd.
Original title: USACOLLE FRIENDS, ICHIGO-USAGI WO SAGASE!
This edition published by arrangement with
Gakken Education Publishing Co. Ltd.
Tokyo, Japan, through PLUS LICENS AB.

First U.S. edition 2011

Library of Congress Cataloging-in-Publication Data is available.
Library of Congress Catalog Card Number 2010038698

ISBN 978-0-7636-5278-4

11 12 13 14 15 16 CCP 10 9 8 7 6 5 4 3 2 1

Printed in Shenzhen, Guangdong, China

This book was typeset in VAG Rounded.
The illustrations were produced digitally.

Candlewick Press, 99 Dover Street, Somerville, Massachusetts 02144

visit us at www.candlewick.com
www.moshimoshikawaii.com

CANDLEWICK PRESS
www.candlewick.com

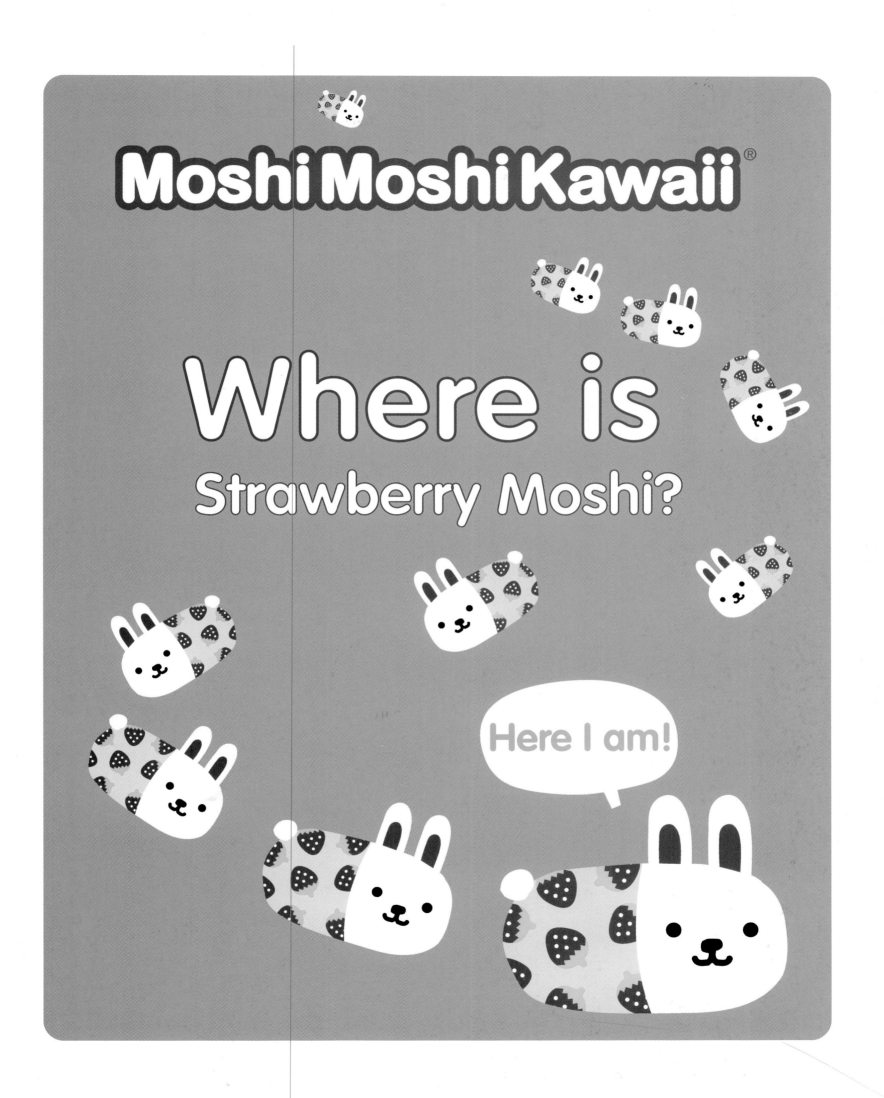

Strawberry Moshi is searching through her closet for her favorite clothes. Can you help her find her outfit decorated with strawberries?

Where is the **strawberry** outfit?

Strawberry Moshi is in **Mushroom Forest**. She is looking for her sweetheart, **Super Moshi**.

Where is **Strawberry Moshi**?

Where is **Super Moshi**?

Find these other Moshi. What are they doing?

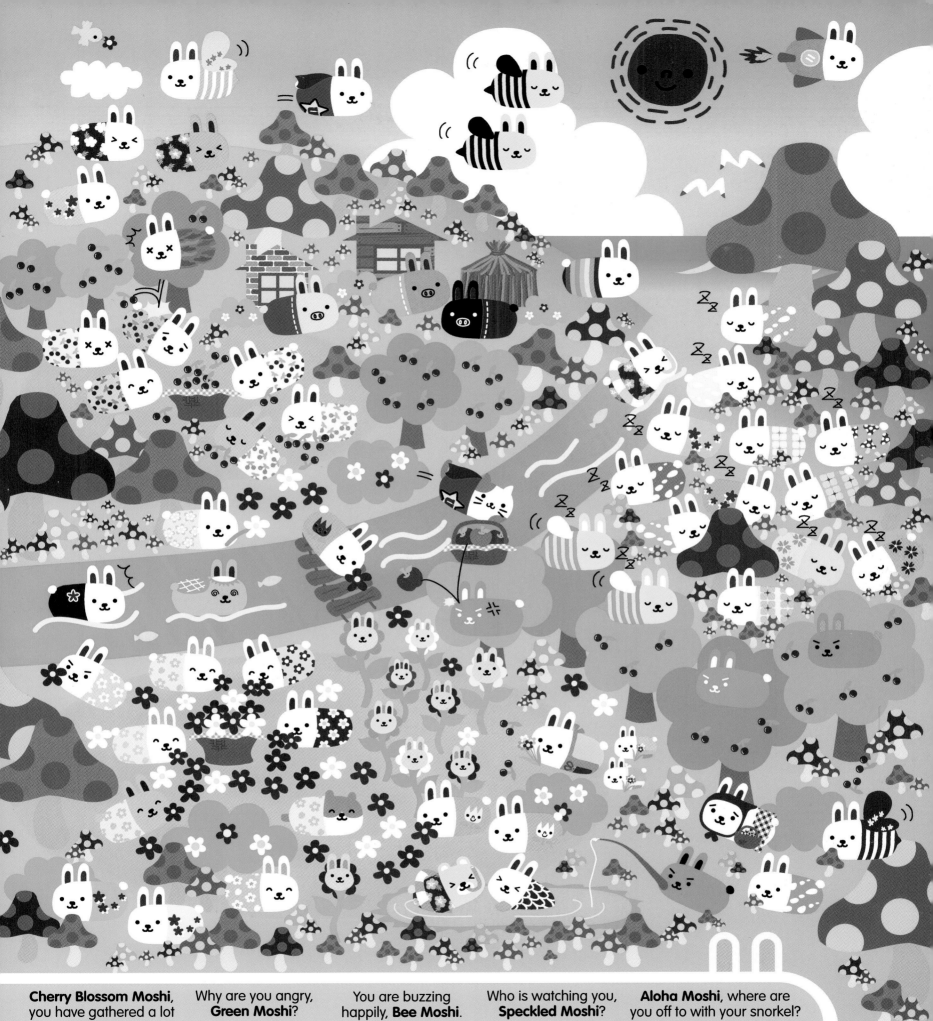

Cherry Blossom Moshi, you have gathered a lot of flowers.

Why are you angry, **Green Moshi**?

You are buzzing happily, **Bee Moshi**.

Who is watching you, **Speckled Moshi**?

Aloha Moshi, where are you off to with your snorkel?

Strawberry Moshi did not find **Super Moshi** in Mushroom Forest, so she has come to **Mermaid Moshi Sea** to look for him.

Where is **Strawberry Moshi?**

Where is **Super Moshi?**

Find these other Moshi. What are they doing?

Mermaid Moshi, you like listening to the sound of the waves.

What are you looking at, **Submarine Moshi**?

Baby Moshi, you can swim like a fish!

Pineapple Moshi, you love the surprises under the sea.

Rainbow Moshi, where are you off to on your surfboard?

START

FINISH

Delicious Land

ICE CREAM

Scary Land

FINISH

Suddenly, a giant **Maze Moshi** pops out of the sea. Find a path through the maze to wonderful **Delicious Land**. But be careful you don't end up in **Scary Land**!

Trace a path through Maze Moshi with your finger. Can you reach Delicious Land?

Strawberry Moshi has arrived in **Delicious Land**, a park where many things are shaped like food. But **Strawberry Moshi** still hasn't found **Super Moshi**.

Where is **Strawberry Moshi**?

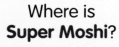

Where is **Super Moshi**?

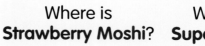

Find these other Moshi. What are they doing?

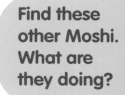

RACING STADIUM

Strawberry Café

ICE CREAM

Star Moshi, you look dizzy!

Is the ice cream good, **Angel Moshi**?

Polka Dot Moshi, is that your boyfriend?

Lovely Moshi, who are you in love with?

Chef Moshi, where are you taking that carrot?

Strawberry Moshi is in **Castle Carrot**, where lots of the Moshi are wearing capes. Will **Strawberry Moshi** be able to find **Super Moshi**?

Where is **Strawberry Moshi**?

Where is **Super Moshi**?

Find these other Moshi. What are they doing?

Princess Moshi, your necklace is beautiful.

Clover Moshi, you look surprised to see your friend.

Sari Moshi, you have a fantastic flying carpet.

Baby Prince Moshi, it's time for your milk!

Don't spill the juice, **Waitress Moshi!**

Menu

Strawberry
Parfait

Carrot Parfait

Strawberry
Juice

Carrot Juice

Hot Strawberry
Milk

Strawberry Moshi has not found
her beloved **Super Moshi** yet. She is
having a snack at **Strawberry Café**
with her friends.

Where is
Strawberry Moshi?

Where is
Super Moshi?

Find these
other Moshi.
What are
they doing?

Isn't the baby cute, **Cherry Moshi**?

Plaid Moshi, watch your step!

Fluffy Moshi, the carrot parfait must taste good.

Thanks for your help, **Silk Moshi**!

Racing Moshi, where are you off to in such in a hurry?

Super Moshi is at the Racing
Stadium, and **Strawberry Moshi**
has come to look for him.
Watch out, racers! *CRASH!*

Where is
Strawberry Moshi?

Where is
Super Moshi?

**Find these
other Moshi.
What are
they doing?**

You're fast, **Robot Moshi**!

Airplane Moshi, spread your wings and fly!

You're nearly there, **Rocket Moshi**!

Bus Moshi, you've still got a chance!

Ambulance Moshi, please hurry up!

START

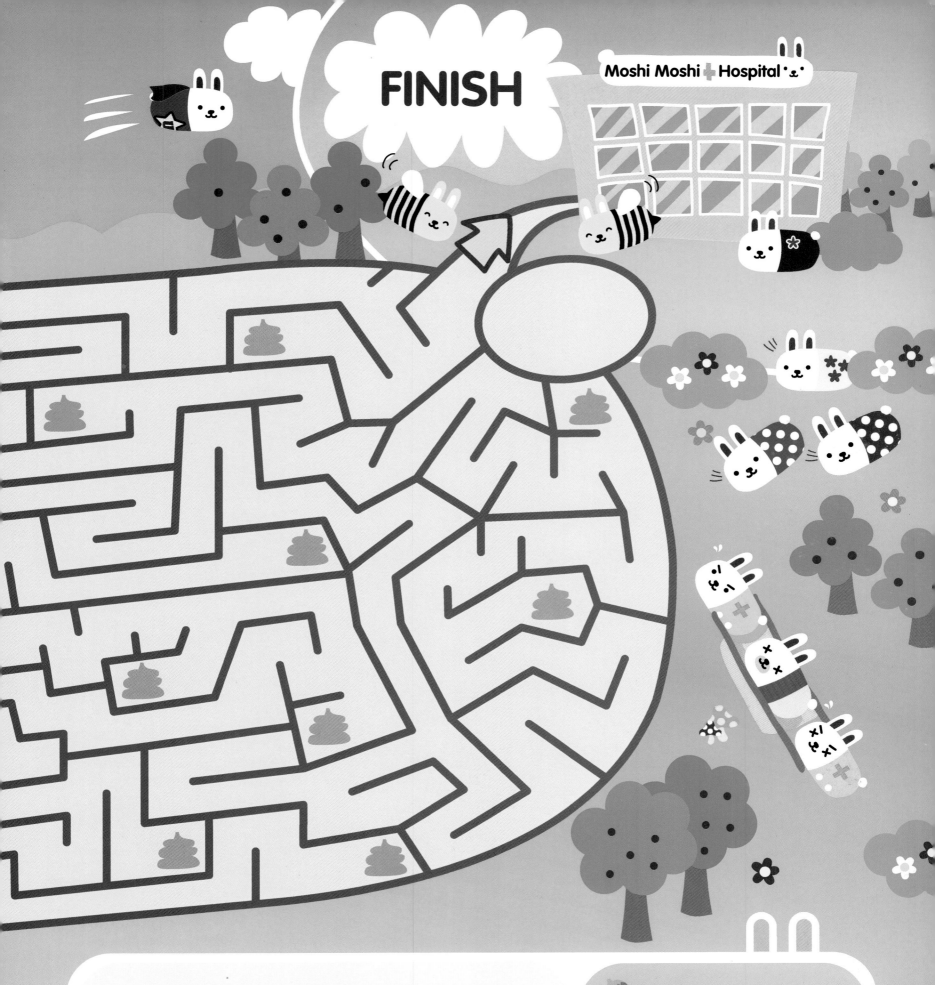

FINISH

Moshi Moshi ✚ Hospital

Ambulance Moshi is rushing the injured Moshi to the hospital. But here is **Maze Moshi** again! They need to quickly find a path through the maze to the hospital.

Find your way through the maze. Watch out for messes on the way!

Moshi Moshi

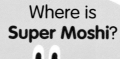

Still searching for **Super Moshi**, **Strawberry Moshi** follows the trail to **Moshi Moshi Hospital**.

Where is **Strawberry Moshi**?

Where is **Super Moshi**?

Find these other Moshi. What are they doing?

Hospital

Injury Moshi, you shouldn't be surprised to be in the hospital.

Flower Moshi, have a good visit with your friends.

Play nicely, **Kindergarten Moshi!**

High School Moshi, how do you feel?

Arabesque Moshi, where are you going with that fan?

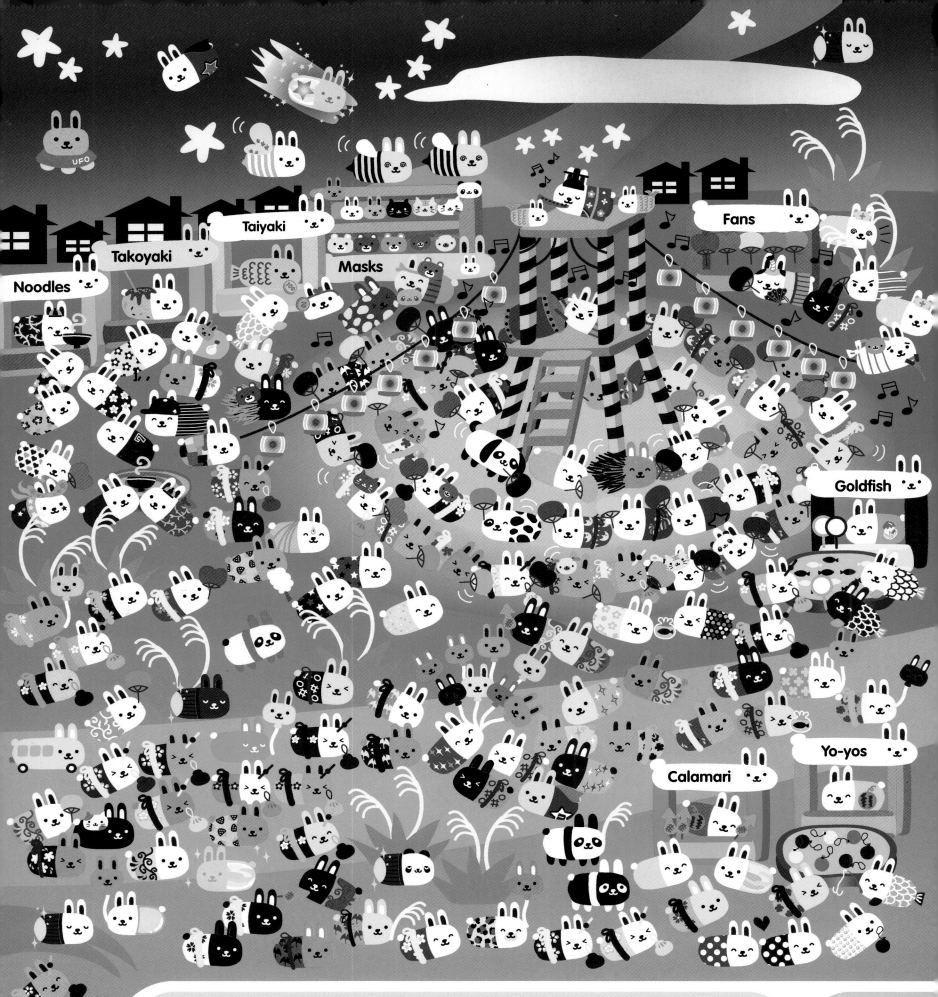

Noodles

Takoyaki

Taiyaki

Masks

Fans

Goldfish

Yo-yos

Calamari

It's evening when **Strawberry Moshi** leaves the hospital. Will **Strawberry Moshi** find **Super Moshi** at the festival on **Moonlight Mountain**?

Where is **Strawberry Moshi**?

Where is **Super Moshi**?

Find these other Moshi. What are they doing?

Cotton Candy

Carrots

Tenmusu

Toys

Sweet Dumplings

Giraffe Moshi, those sweet dumplings look good.

Hedgehog Moshi, you are a very good dancer.

What are you looking at, **Fish Moshi?**

Panda Moshi, you must be having fun at the festival.

Light up the night, **Firefly Moshi!**

Keep on searching!

Here are even more Moshi to find. Look again at each scene to see if you can spot them.

This is **Oyaji Moshi.** He is in every scene.
Follow his story through from the beginning.

Mushroom Forest

Mermaid Moshi Sea

Maze Moshi

Delicious Land

Castle Carrot

Strawberry Café

Racing Stadium

Maze Moshi

Moshi Moshi Hospital

Moonlight Mountain

And look again for these Moshi and their trinkets.

Mushroom Forest

Kappa Moshi

Three Little Pig Moshi

Wicked Witch Moshi

Little Samurai Moshi

Red Riding Hood Moshi

Mermaid Moshi Sea

Moshi Sea Otter

Moshi Taiyaki

Moshi Hermit Crab

Moshi Whale

Moshi Banjo

Delicious Land

Moshi Mail Box

Moshi Purse

Camera Moshi

Moshi Balloon

Moshi Bench

Castle Carrot

King Moshi

Tuxedo Moshi

Knight Moshi

Present Moshi

Cleaning Moshi

Strawberry Café

Cake Moshi

Moshi Cookies

Moshi Shaved Ice

Moshi Pudding

Moshi Baby Bottle

Racing Stadium

Moshi UFO

Moshi Cell Phone

Firecracker Moshi

Moshi Onigiri

Moshi Battery Charger

UFO

BATTERY CHARGER

Moshi Moshi Hospital

Moshi Bandage

Moshi Syringe

Radio Moshi

Moshi Pillow

Moshi Plant

Moonlight Mountain

Flute Player Moshi

Sumo Moshi

Shooting Star Moshi

Tenmusu Moshi

Takoyaki Moshi

Keep on searching for Strawberry Moshi in

MoshiMoshiKawaii®
Where is Strawberry Princess Moshi?

A Strawberry Moshi game book
It's cute, it's fun!

and also in
Where is Strawberry Mermaid Moshi?

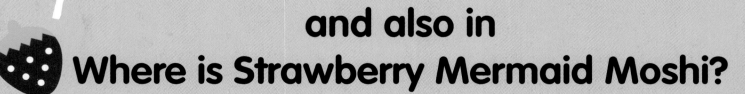